This Book Belongs To:

_____

The Tale of the Selfish Shellfish

Sharon Lee

AuthorHouse™ UK Ltd.
500 Avebury Boulevard
Central Milton Keynes, MK9 2BE
www.authorhouse.co.uk
Phone: 08001974150

First published by AuthorHouse   4/1/2011

ISBN: 978-1-4567-7697-8 (sc)

Any people depicted in stock imagery provided by Thinkstock are models,
and such images are being used for illustrative purposes only.
Certain stock imagery © Thinkstock.

This book is printed on acid-free paper.

Because of the dynamic nature of the Internet, any web addresses or links contained in this book may have changed
since publication and may no longer be valid. The views expressed in this work are solely those of the author and do not
necessarily reflect the views of the publisher, and the publisher hereby disclaims any responsibility for them.

authorHOUSE®

Down at the bottom of the deep, blue sea
lived a mean old lobster, as selfish as could be.
He never helped any of his sea-dwelling friends,
his moaning and selfishness knew no ends.

This lobster thought he was the King of the Ocean
but sadly this King showed no caring emotion.
He thought the sea creatures that shared his sea-floor
were a nuisance to him, nothing less, nothing more.

One day as lobster took a stroll by the docks
he heard a faint cry from somewhere in the rocks.
As he got nearer he saw a big conga eel
who was caught in a fishing net, you should have heard him squeal!

'Please help me Mr Lobster' the eel cried out in fright
'I've been trapped in here for hours, I won't make it through the night.
I've had nothing to eat you see and I can't swim away,
so please help me, Mr Lobster, see another day'.

But Mr Lobster wasn't friendly and he said: 'It's not my fault
that you chose to rest somewhere where fishes have been caught.
Yes, my strong claws may break the net and help you to get free,
but if they get tangled in the fishing net, where will that leave me?'

And off he went on his way, as poor eel watched him go;
'Lord help that Lobster' prayed the eel, 'He really ought to know,
that you should help others in need whenever the chance may be
for you never know when the tide will turn - he might need help
from me!'

As lobster went on his way, feeling big and grand
he came across some mussels playing music in the sand.
'Hey, Mr Lobster, could you help us out?
We need some claws for our band' they began to shout.

But selfish Mr Lobster, he didn't want to know
'Of course not, silly mussels, I'm busy and have to go'.
'That mean old nasty lobster' sniffed a mussel with a sob,
'we only needed a bit of help, he could have done the job'.

'We think he needs teaching a lesson' agreed the mussels' friends
'if only there were some way we could get him to make amends'.
Little did the mussels know as they played their music and danced,
that in a very short time they would get the perfect chance.

The mussels danced the night away as the sea turned inky black and once the sunlight vanished they snapped their shells with a 'clack'! Then other small sea creatures went to hide and sleep in the dark because once the night-time falls on the sea, it's feeding time for the sharks!

As the waters around the eel grew dark and daylight began to fade, he thought how lobster should have saved him, he was so dismayed. So when two swordfish swam towards him he was quite confounded and when they sawed through the net with their swords – my, he was astounded!

The net that was trapping him ripped apart as if was cut with a knife;
as soon as he saw that tear appear, he quickly swam for his life.
Two strangers had come and set him free, he couldn't believe his luck;
from now on he vowed he'd help anyone, he was so awestruck!

As dawn broke over the ocean and the suns rays fell on the sea, the waters warmed, the fish came out and everyone swam free. One of the mussels decided to swim down to the fields of fresh kelp and on his way there he heard a funny noise – it sounded a bit like 'Help'!

He crept a bit closer and you'll never guess what he saw?
He wasn't sure himself, he'd seen nothing like it before.
A basket, a bit like a fishing net, only solid and firm
and on the ropes of the basket were some wiggly worms.

The noise from the basket was quite loud and frightening,
cracking and thrashing, the noises sounded like lightning.
For inside the basket who was snapping his claws?
It was old Mr Lobster – trying to find the baskets flaws.

Well the mussel could see why lobster was so distressed
'But I'm not strong enough to help you' the mussel confessed.
'Then go away and leave me trapped in here to die'
Snapped the lobster angrily – then he started to cry.

As soon as he saw the peril lobster was in
Mussel made up his mind 'I must help him begin
to smash through this cage of rope, wicker and cane,
so lobster can escape his trap and swim free again'.

The mussel clamped hard on a small rope swinging free
and with all his might he pulled but the rope was slippery.
It slipped through his shell and he fell over backwards
then suddenly the basket started moving slowly upwards.

They both looked up and saw the horrible shadow of a boat,
as they realised what the trap was, a lump formed in their throats.
Mussel swam around the trap biting cane here and there
then suddenly there were little mussels all around – everywhere!

And not only mussels but who else did swim by?
The very same eel that lobster left trapped to die!
Said eel, 'now hold on, just what's this commotion?
Oh, look – it's mean lobster, the King of the Ocean'!

'Don't worry though lobster, I'll try to get you free,
I'll be kinder to you than you were to me.
I'm a better man you see, I won't bear a grudge,
so stand well back lobster, I'll give it a nudge'!

Then eel threw himself at the basket of terror
but avoided the top, he wouldn't make the same error.
He flicked and banged the basket with his thick, strong, tail,
using all his strength to try to free lobster from his jail.

Then the eel and the mussels quickly formed a big queue,
Eel had seen a weak spot in the trap and knew just what to do!
Keeping the door shut was a rope and an old rusty lock;
they latched on to this rope, began to pull and began to rock.

With eel's size and strength and the mussels assistance
their efforts became fruitful thanks to dogged persistence.
They could see the old lock was beginning to weaken;
the wicker in the basket was beginning to creak, and

after almost a minute of tugging and bashing
the lock finally broke and lobster tumbled out, thrashing!
The mussels, eel and lobster fell together to the sea-bed,
'oh, however can I thank you' the grateful lobster said.

'I am truly sorry I was mean to you before
if it wasn't for you all I'd now be on the sea shore'.
'It doesn't matter now' young mussel kindly replied,
'that's all in the past, so let's leave that aside'.

'We might be small and tiny but we have our uses
we're called mussels for a reason – and that's no excuse!'
Mr Lobster sat and rubbed his claws, getting himself together,
'from now on', he slowly said, 'we'll be friends forever'!

So the eel, lobster and mussels formed a new music band with lobster as the drummer; they were 'Muscles in the Sand'. And lobster found his new life being pleasant was such fun that never again was he selfish or mean to anyone!

The End

Lightning Source UK Ltd.
Milton Keynes UK
UKIC02n0303140616
276256UK00013B/64